MW01248185

Whispers in the Dark is a work of fiction. Names, characters, places, and incidents either are the product of the author's imagination or are used fictitiously. Any resemblance to actual persons, living or dead, events or locales is entirely coincidental.

Whispers in the Dark

Jason R. Cash

Chapter 1

The Story Begins

"Grab A can of that wood polish, Daniel."

Daniel reaches over and slaps the back of Dennis's head, returning what his brother had done to him. Then, trotting over to the wood polish, he picks up a can, as his mother had asked.

Daniel and Dennis are twin brothers; Daniel is the oldest by eight and a half minutes. He is named after his father, but his father goes by Dan. Though they are twins, they are not identical twins. In fact, they don't look like twins at all. Daniel has light brown hair that is so thin that when he moves, his hair sways like waves in the ocean. His face is covered in freckles, and he was given not-so-perfect eyesight. He has been wearing glasses since the age of two. Daniel is the type that has read more books than seen movies. His knowledge of science is very strong; since early education, he has loved science. He is outgoing around people he knows but quiet around those he doesn't know.

Dennis is the opposite; He has darker brown curly hair. His skin does not show one mark of a freckle, and he doesn't wear glasses.

Dennis is more than outgoing; he is more like an overachiever for attention. If his twin brother is grabbing attention, Dennis will always find something to do to either make his brother's attention negative or turn it around towards him.

If Daniel had the attention on him with a good grade in class or something along those lines, Dennis would turn it around and mention to his parents and whoever else was there how his brother got in trouble for something. In return, his parents would forget about the good grades and start asking about the incident that got him in trouble.

On other occasions, he would turn the attention around by saying something about his brother to make friends laugh at him. He was jealous and didn't like being in second place behind his eight-and-a-half-minute older brother, Daniel.

Dennis couldn't care less about school. He was okay with getting a good enough grade to advance to the next grade.

"Did you see that mom? He just hit me!" Dennis shouts to his mother.

"Dennis, if I remember correctly, you had just done that to him seconds before," their mother firmly says.

The twin boy's mother, Karen Matthews, wasn't a strict by-the-rules mother. But she tried as much as she could to keep them in place. She and her husband, Dan, have been married for fifteen years. Just one year before the boys entered this world. She is a whopping 5'2; the boys already tower over her. With that said, though, her stern voice keeps them in line, and the boys always know when they hear her voice that she means business. Her husband Dan, who is on the other side of the store looking at sports magazines, is a sports writer for their local newspaper. If anyone took after him, it was undoubtedly Daniel, who had glasses and excellent grades in school.

"Come on, boys, let's go find your father so we can check out, get to the house, and get to work."

Two months earlier, Karen's aunt passed away. Karen was the only one left in her family who was still living and was given the house through her aunt's will. Karen didn't know her aunt too well; their family grew up and lost touch. The only one still living, Karen was awarded all her aunt's belongings. Since her aunt died, Karen has been in a mood. They live 700 miles away from where her aunt lived. She was not in the best mood between having her and Dan take time off work and driving out there. She and Dan made good money and had nice things; she tried to get the bank to sell the house and everything in it, but they refused. She called shelters and tried to donate the house, but no one wanted it. Some places she called even had a shivery voice after they found out which house it was, and then they would hang up on her. Having to come down to take control of the house, she was more intrigued by why everyone seemed scared of the house.

"Ok, boys, help me get this stuff on the belt," Karen asks as the clerk starts ringing up their merchandise.

Halfway through emptying the grocery cart, the boys start picking at each other again and knock over a magazine rack.

"Boys!" Karen shouts. Are you going to do anything about this?" she asks Dan and turns to face him.

Dan was standing there still reading the sports magazine.

"What? What are they doing?" Dan asks while continuing to read. After a moment, he lowers the magazine and looks at the boys. "Do as your mother told you to do." Then, he raises the magazine and continues where he had left off.

Karen sighed with frustration and finished unloading the grocery cart herself.

Walking out of the grocery store and towards their car with the sun's heat bearing down on them made the moment's mood even worse.

"I can't see how anyone would want to live in this heat!" Karen says, pushing past the boys and Dan with the cart.

It was much hotter here in Macon, Georgia than where they were from. Dan and Karen were born and raised in Cleveland, Ohio, which has a much different climate.

"When we both go back to school, all we will have to tell our friends about the things we did this summer was sweat our asses off," Dennis whispers to Daniel.

"What was that!" Karen shouts, leaning out of the vehicle as she loads the groceries.

"Nothing, Mother," Dennis says and jumps in the back seat, trying to get away from her.

"Dan! Do something about his mouth!"

"Dennis." Dan shouts, "Watch your mouth."

Dan gets into the car's front seat and waits for Karen to push the buggy into the designated spot and climb into the car.

With an angry sigh, Karen slams the cart into the cart holder and then jumps into the car, slamming the door as well. She has had a growing problem with the way her husband disciplines the boys for quite some time now — or lack of discipline, that is. After arguing with him over and over about it, he still hasn't changed.

Chapter 2

The Neighborhood

"When we get there, I want everyone to help me with everything in the trunk," Karen says, knowing that if she didn't say anything, they wouldn't offer to help.

Just like all children do, theirs followed in their father's footsteps. When they were younger, they would love to help their mother with everything she did. Now, a little older, they watch their father, and seeing that he doesn't help her with anything, they start following in his footsteps and quit helping her, too.

Looking out the window, Dennis watches as the town passes by. It is more of a lower-class city than where they were from. He was used to seeing two and three-story houses and a pool in every backyard with a two-car garage. He wasn't used to seeing trailer parks and low-cost apartment complexes. He was used to neatly combed yards, not wild grass growing out of control, and some yards looking like they hadn't been mowed in weeks.

In his town, people walked on the sidewalks, but none of them pushed shopping carts with their whole lives inside them. It was a different world here, miles away from home, and Dennis was already getting the chills before they even reached the house.

"When your father and I tell you, you don't know how good you two have it. This is what we're talking about, with a nice roof over your head and all the things you've ever wanted." Karen tells the twin boys as they ride past a half-burnt-down trailer with a camper in the front yard, possibly where the people live until their home is repaired.

"The scenery and the way of life here will be a little different from back home."

Both boys agree as they look in disbelief out their windows at the city.

"Is this what Aunt Isabelle's house is going to look like?" Daniel asks, shaky as if he doesn't want to know the answer.

"No, Daniel. It is an older neighborhood, so the houses are older, but they look nicer." She says, looking back towards him in the backseat. He sits there looking nervous.

The twins have been sheltered in their lives. Their parents wanted the finer things in life, so they neglected to show them the not-so-fine things. This is their first time seeing rural developments. When they would go to their favorite restaurants in the town, their parents would drive miles out of the way on the interstate to bypass the areas they didn't want to take their kids through.

"Here we are, Shady Estates," Karen informs the boys. "Are we ready to get this house clean and straightened so we can get back on the road and back home?"

"The sooner, the better!" Both boys said simultaneously.

Dan turns into the neighborhood, looking around at the houses.
"Which one is it?" He asks Karen.

"It is the very last house on the right." She says, looking around. "I was only here once for Christmas when I was eleven. It is funny how you can only visit a place once years ago, but when you return, it feels like it was just yesterday." She looks out the window with a smile on her face.

"I didn't want to come all the way here, but now that we are here and I am seeing this place again, all the memories from that Christmas are coming back. This is where I met the first boy I had a crush on."

"How many of them were there?" Dan asks with a look of interest on his face.

"Oh, stop. You were the one I ended up marrying." Turning back to the window, she says to herself, "Unfortunately."

Driving through the neighborhood, they all look out the window as they pass each house, with different people living their lives. Two children jump on a trampoline as a man sprays the lawn hose, cooling them off in the hot southern air. Across the street, a younger teenage boy helps an elderly man into the house. As the old man enters the house, the young man pats him on the back. Down the street, a middle-aged woman is checking her mail. Just by looking at each house, it is apparent that it is a quiet neighborhood where people leave each day in peace and safety. But what these neighbors don't know yet is that the people driving through are about to unlock the horror and mystery that this neighborhood has tried so hard to forget.

They reach the house they have driven so far to clean and prepare to sell. It is an older ranch-style home with an open garage. The front yard looks close to half an acre, with the backyard at least two acres. The grass has grown over four feet high, and the mailbox has been knocked down and beaten in, lying in the driveway.

"It looks like you boys will cut the grass first thing in the morning," their mother said as she looked in the back seat, smiling at them.

The four get out of the car and start unpacking the trunk. Daniel looks around and stands there, halting all movements.

"What is it?" Dennis asks.

The four of them look around at the neighborhood; everyone in the neighborhood who was once doing their own thing as they drove by is now doing the same thing. They are staring at them as they unpack their car. Some of them have grouped, and you can see them talking to each other as they look at each other. You can hear whispers; some of them holding their hands up to their mouths as if they couldn't believe someone was getting out at that house.

"What's going on?" Dan asks Karen.

"I don't know." She says as she closes the trunk of the car. "Let's go in and get started."

As they walk towards the door, you can hear the talking happening in the neighborhood. They are far away enough not to make out what they are saying, but you can hear them.

Opening the front door to the house, it was as if they found the key to a long-lost junk pile. The house was destroyed on the inside. Clothes were thrown all over the floor, shelves were knocked over, and lying on the floor. As soon as they walked in, they smelt a foul stench of old food, dirty clothes, and a musky smell like sweat. The power had been turned off until Karen called ahead and turned it back on. Whoever was there last had turned the thermostat off, so the house was very hot and humid. The heat mixing with the smell just amplified everything even more.

"Your aunt didn't live too healthy, did she?" Dad asks as he leaps over half of a tray of pizza turned over on the floor and almost entirely rotten away.

"She wasn't like this always, they told me. Towards her last years of life, she started going crazy.

Daniel and Dennis had made their way into the bedrooms to look around. Dennis found something and rushed it down to his parents immediately.

"Mom! Dad! Look at this!" He says, jumping over a pile of clothes.

His mother takes the picture out of his hands, a photo of her Uncle with a little girl. Someone had driven a knife into the picture where her uncle's heart was.

"Who is this in the picture? They never had any children." Karen says.

Everything was quiet as all four stood there looking at the picture.

Suddenly, someone bangs on the front door, making all four of them almost jump out of their skin. Dan goes to the door to answer it.

"Hello, sorry to bother you; I am from the power company. I am just making sure everything is working properly."

"Yes," Karen turns and says to the man as Dan holds the door open. Everything is working fine. Thanks again for turning it on so promptly for us."

"Yes, ma'am, not a problem." The guy peers into the house with noticeable shakes going through his body. "So, did you and your family purchase this house?" He asks, looking at Dan.

"No, it was my wife's Aunt's house; we are here to straighten it up and get it ready to sell."

"Oh, okay." He says, looking into the house suspiciously like he was waiting for something or someone to jump out at any minute and scare the five of them. "I better be getting back to the station. Call us and let us know if you have any power problems."

"We will, thanks," Dan says as he shuts the door. "Why is everyone acting so strange towards us? I know we aren't from around here, but why all the looks? I thought they were supposed to show southern hospitality?"

Karen laughs at the thought of Southern hospitality and points to all the junk on the living room floor. "Well, let's get started on this room so we can have a floor to sleep on tonight."

Dennis glances out the window and sees the whole neighborhood staring towards the house.

They were talking amongst each other. One more person joined the conversations outside. The man from the power company was out there talking with everyone in the crowd.

"What is going on here?" Dennis asks himself as he closes the curtains and helps the rest of the family clean up.

After fifteen bags of trash, old clothes were thrown from the living room floor into the garage to be bagged later, dishes and other miscellaneous things were organized and put in designated boxes, and they finally cleaned the living room well enough to sleep for the night.

The twins and Dan are straightening up the kitchen while their mother prepares their supper for the night. They did not know what utensils they would have or the condition of the kitchen, so they purchased plastic utensils.

They bought easy foods to prepare for the first few days of their stay. Their mother was cooking spaghetti as she washed the dirty dishes left behind by her late aunt.

"After we straighten the rooms, we will turn around and pack the things that are either still good or handed down through generations to take back with us.

"With the furniture, we will either have a yard sale or give it to the Salvation Army," Karen says while washing the dishes.

"Look at this!" Dan says, holding up a picture.

It was another picture with her Uncle and the little girl. In this picture, he lifts her as she holds a basketball. In the foreground, you can see the goal to which she throws the ball.

Looking at the second picture, Karen still can't figure out who this little girl is. They never had children; her aunt was not able to have kids. They did not have any nieces; the only thing she could figure out was maybe a friend of the family's kid or maybe a neighborhood kid.

"Put it on the counter," Karen says as she returns to the sink to finish the dishes.

Having finished the cups and dishes, she was now down to the last few pots and pans; reaching in, she grabbed a pot. As she raises the pot to eye level, she looks into the reflection at her puffy eyes; she needs some rest. She hadn't slept much a few days before the trip because she always gets nervous before traveling. Looking deeper into her face, she remembers that Christmas here and sees how much she has grown since then. It seems like millenniums ago until she returned to the neighborhood; now that she is back in familiar surroundings, it seems like it was yesterday.

"Whatever happened to Ronnie?" She thinks to herself. "Was he successful in life? Did he get married and have kids? Does he still live in this town?" Then she thinks to herself about worse scenarios. "Is he still alive? Did he end up in the lower-class neighborhood?" Referring to the neighborhood they had passed through on the way to her aunt's house.

Standing there, she looks into the pot and recalls old memories.

An image passes by, and seeing it in the reflection of the pot, she screams. Turning around quickly, she discovers nothing is there.

"What is it!" Dan shouts as he and the twins rush to her aid.

Karen looks at them as if she saw a ghost. "I." She stops to catch her breath. "I just, I think I just saw."

"What? What did you see?" Dan asks eagerly, wanting to know what is wrong.

"That…That little girl from the picture. I could have sworn I just saw her walk by!" She says, motioning with her finger, showing where the reflection had come from.

"The little girl? You couldn't have." Dan assures her. "The only ones here are me and the boys."

"I know, but I just saw someone walk by, and the last time I checked, the boys don't wear dresses!"

The twins stand there in horror. "Mom, you're scaring me!" Daniel says, wide-eyed at the look on his mother's face.

"Me too!" Dennis assures them.

"Honey, I think it's time for you to lay down. You are overtired and need to rest." Dan tells her as he takes her hand and walks into the living room. Laying her down on the couch, he leans in and kisses her.

"Just lay down and rest; I will finish the supper and let you know when it's ready."

Karen doesn't complain about the invitation to rest. She lies down on the couch and closes her eyes as Dan and the twins finish making supper. It was nice for a change for the men to take over in charge and let her rest. It was what she had wanted her husband to start doing for a long time. She thought, "This could be the beginning of changes in our family I have wanted for the past few years."

Those thoughts moved out, and the thoughts of the room came in; her thoughts were wondering like they usually do with someone who is overtired. Her thoughts now were upon the room she was lying in. The room smelled of mothballs, which is one smell she remembered from childhood when she came to the house. The couch had a smell of mildew and dog hair. She remembered her Aunt having a lot of dogs. It was the same couch her aunt had since that Christmas. Looking at the walls were pictures; one picture was of her uncle when he was in the army. In those days, he had a head full of black hair, a trimmed mustache, and a clean-cut face. The only visual she remembered of her uncle was when he was much older. Then he had thin, balding gray hair, no mustache or beard, and wore glasses. Adjacent to that picture was a wedding photo; her aunt was much thinner in that picture. Her age brought upon weight as well; it was the only time she ever saw a smile on her aunt's face in that picture. In other pictures, she had smiles, but they were more like smirks. Like something was always on her mind bothering her. When Karen was around her, she never saw her smile or in a happy mood; she would always sit silently as the family get-togethers went by without truly smiling once.

Karen's eyes get so weak that she can hardly keep them open. A few seconds later, she was asleep on the couch.

Dan walks in to let her know supper is ready; seeing her asleep, he leaves her alone. Dan and the boys eat supper, then camp in sleeping bags beside their mother in the living room for the night.

Chapter 3

Sleepless Night

The night is quiet; Daniel lies there, unable to sleep. Looking at his wristwatch, he can see the time by the moon shining a single ray through a crack in the blinds. It is one-thirty in the morning, and he is still awake. His body is tired from the earlier visions of the neighbors staring at them and the moment his mother sees a reflection of someone. He was terrified to close his eyes and lower his guard for rest.

Daniel rises, rubbing his eyes. He looks around the room at his family sleeping. With his bladder feeling as if it was about to burst, he gets up to go to the restroom. After he is done, he looks into the mirror at his bloodshot eyes. He is tired and needs to get some sleep. Reaching towards the wall, he turns the bathroom light off and steps back into the hall towards the living room, where his sleeping bag is waiting for him.

"Help me!"

A whisper that sounded like it came from a female child.

Daniel stops in his tracks, "Who was that?" He asks himself, his heart racing faster than a set of drums at a rock concert. Returning to the bathroom, he turns the light on and looks around. No one was there; only his family was asleep in the living room. "I need some sleep." He says to himself as he turns the light off. "I'm hearing things now." He says, knowing he was way overtired. Stepping over his brother slowly and quietly, trying not to wake him, he slips back into his sleeping bag. Lying there, he closes his eyes finally to let the sleep take hold of him for the night.

"Help!"

Daniel springs his eyes open; he hears the voice again. Lying there, wide-eyed and very still, he hears the voice whisper, "Help me," once more.

Daniel pulls the cover over his face; his heart is racing uncontrollably.
"Calm down, you're hearing things." He says to himself.

"Nothing to be afraid of; it's your imagination."

Earlier, he didn't think he was going to sleep that night; now, he knew he wasn't going to sleep at all.

Daniel hears movement, and his whole body starts to tremble. There are a few seconds of silence, and then he hears the movement again. He is shaking so hard now that his teeth begin to chatter.

A third time, there was movement; something brushed up against his foot.

Daniel jumps out of the sleeping bag, screaming. Looking down to where his foot once was in the sleeping bag, he sees his brother rolling over beside him and brushing his foot against him. Taking a deep breath of relief, he climbs back into his bed on the floor for the night.

"Boy, what are you screaming about?"

Daniel's heart almost jumped into his throat; his heart was again racing. It suddenly stopped when he looked up and saw his father sitting up, talking to him.

"We have a long day tomorrow; lay down and get some sleep."

"Yes, sir," Daniel replies, laying his head back on his pillow. He could only lie down; he didn't sleep that night. He lay there, keeping his guard up from whatever was coming next.

Karen woke up the next morning to the smell of bacon and eggs. Raising up, she looked at the clock. It was six-thirty in the morning. Dennis was the only one still lying there asleep.

"Good morning, honey." She hears Dan say as he sits beside her on the couch. "You hungry?"

Dan sets a tray in front of her; he cooked bacon, eggs, and toast and made her a glass of orange juice.

"You were asleep before supper was ready last night; you must be hungry."

Still half asleep, she looks up at Dan. "Thanks," she says with a smile as she grabs the glass of orange juice and drinks. "I am starving."

Dennis rises from his sleeping bag and sees his mother and father sitting on the couch eating.

"Good morning, Dennis; your breakfast is in the kitchen."

Walking into the kitchen, he grabs his plate from the counter and sits across from his brother at the table.

"You look like crap." He whispers to Daniel low enough so his parents won't hear his choice of words.

Daniel looks up at him and then starts eating again.

"What's wrong with you?" He asks, pushing for answers.

Daniel takes a drink and then looks back at his brother. "There is something in this house."

"Yeah, a bunch of crap that we have to clean up," Dennis says with a smile as he brings a fork full of eggs to his mouth.

"No! I mean something not of this world. A ghost or something!"

"A ghost; you see things like mom did last night? You wouldn't see these things if the two of you got some rest."

Daniel stares at his brother with an evil look.
"That is not it; I heard a voice last night. It kept saying help me over and over."

"Daniel, there is nothing in this house. Mom didn't see anything, and you weren't hearing anything. We have been in this house for one night, and the two of you are so homesick already that it is driving you two crazy." Dennis tells him as he gets up from the table and lays his dirty plate into the sink. "You two should have just stayed home and let the two men come down here and clean this pigsty up."

Chapter 4

History of the House

"Let's get started in the guest room; then we will all clean the master bedroom," Karen says, eager to end this ordeal so they can all go home.

Walking into the guest room, their hopes of leaving early slowly diminish.

"We will be in this room alone for three weeks," Daniel says, disgusted at the mess.

There were boxes upon boxes thrown everywhere; in between

the boxes were loose papers and other trash.

"The longer we stand here, the longer it will take," Dan says, urging them to get moving.

The twins start in the left corner of the room, while Karen and Dan start on the right-hand side. In the first box, the boys opened were old clothes that were getting frail. Karen also opens a box full of clothes. Some clothes were ripping in their hands as they took them out of the boxes. Rising from the floor, Karen opens the window.

"All the boxes of trash will be thrown out the window. Then, when we are finished, we load them up and take them off. But for now, throw them into the yard to free up the space in the bedroom."

Daniel and Karen both throw each box out onto the lawn. Peering out the window, he sees two little girls jumping rope. The girls hear the boxes crash as they hit the ground. Like yesterday, they look over and start staring at their every move.

"This neighborhood creeps me out," Daniel says, moving away from the window. "Why do they keep staring at us, Mom?"

"I don't know, son. I am wondering the same thing. They all give me the creeps," she says as a chill runs down her spine.

"Did something happen in this house that we don't know about?" Dennis adds as he opens

the second box, which also
contains clothes.

"How did your uncle die?"
Dan asks, ripping another box
open.

"Well, it happened when I
was still young. I think I was
around fifteen." She says, taking a
seat on the floor. "It was around
Easter. I remember coming home
with your grandma after buying
my new dress. Your grandpa was
on the phone, and we heard him
say, "How did it happen?" He
looked at your grandma with a
frown and motioned for her to
approach him. Then, as you would
suspect, she fell to the floor crying.
They told her that her brother died
by falling and breaking his neck.

"Aunt Mary said he got out of bed and tripped over the chest at the foot of the bed. He fell over and hit his head on the fireplace, and it broke his neck. Uncle John had surgery on his leg when he was in the war. He was shot in the leg, and the doctors had trouble resetting the bone. Then, while he was recovering from that injury, they were relocating him to another hospital outside of the war zone. The vehicle that was transporting him was attacked. In the wreck, that same leg was broken in three more places. After all the surgeries to reset it, he was left with a permanent limp. That night, she said his bad leg tripped over the chest."

"He had a gunshot wound, then it was broken in a wreck?" Dennis asks with a cringe of pain on his face. "I can't even imagine that. Ouch!" He pauses to let it all sink in, "Then that leg is what killed him by tripping over the chest."

"So what happened to Aunt Mary?" Daniel urges, wanting to keep memory lane going.

"Aunt Mary? They found her sitting at the table with her head down. She had passed away, they said, two to three days earlier. The mailman had a package for her; knocking on the kitchen side door, he saw her sitting there and not answering. He decided to walk in and found out she was dead."

"They said she stopped breathing, no heart attack or anything else. Her body shut down, and she stopped breathing."

Everyone sat quietly for a moment; I think they had enough of the memory lane and talking of death in the house where they sat.

"This room," Karen adds, trying to make the subject more positive. "This is the room where I stayed that Christmas we were here. There was a bed there." Pointing to the far corner where more boxes were stacked. "That's where mom and dad slept; I slept beside them on the floor. I remember that Christmas because that was the first trip we ever took outside of Ohio. I thought it was so cool to be in another state; it was like being in another country to me." Karen rips open another box of old clothes and throws it out the window. "Oh well, enough of memory lane. Let's get this house cleaned so we can get back home."

Everyone agrees and starts going through the boxes.

They continue to open boxes and throw the old, tattered, torn clothes out the window. "She had a lot of clothes," Daniel says, sitting in front of boxes.

"Yes," Karen starts. "I believe her house could be on that TV show. The one about hoarding."

"I agree," Dennis says, ripping another box open.

Raising the clothes out of the box, Dennis looks at his mother and then at Daniel and thinks about when his mother said she saw a reflection of a little girl. Then

Daniel said he heard a girl's voice last night.

He stares at the clothes in his hand; they are little girl's clothes.

"Mom?" Dennis says, holding them up. "Whose clothes are these?"

Karen stood up immediately; it was the same blue dress with white trim around the dress's arms, neck, and bottom.

Pointing at the dress with her right hand while covering her mouth with her left. "That was the dress I saw in the reflection!"

Daniel stands up with her, looking at his mother. Then, back at the dress in his brother's hands.

Daniel takes the dress out of Dennis's hands and throws it back in the box, then throws the box out of the window. "Let's get those clothes out of here!"

Looking back at his brother, Dennis opens the following box. It was also young girls' clothing.

He pulled a beige blouse out of the box, and all four saw a hole in the side of the blouse and a dark stain around it.

Karen looks at her husband, Dan. He takes the shirt out of Dennis's hand, puts it in the box, and then takes the box downstairs and sets it by the front door.

Walking outside, Dan gets a breath of fresh air. The house had his nostrils swollen from the smells. After a sneezing fit earlier, his nose was enjoying the freshness of the current air.

He walks around the house through the tall grass and picks up the other box of girls' clothing they had found. He picked up the fallen garments and saw a pair of old jeans with similar stains.

Walking back towards the front porch, one of the children jumping on the trampoline ran up to get a closer look.

"That house is evil!" She shouts to Dan.

He turns to her and asks what she is talking about, but the girl has already returned to where her friends are on the trampoline.

Dan returns to the house and sets the boxes on top of each other. "We need to find out where these clothes came from," he says to Karen.

She nodded in agreement, "Yeah, but let's complete the house first."

After going through the boxes, they cleaned the remaining things off the floor. Old photo albums were scattered everywhere. Along with newspapers, the carpet was so worn that it would have to be replaced. The smell of animal dander and feces was so strong that they could not sit on it while going through everything. They had to bring chairs from the kitchen into the room. The smell stuck to their fingers as they picked everything off the floor, making them sick.

"I can't do much more of this, mama," Daniel says, looking at his hands in disgust.

"Why don't the two of you go wash up? Daddy and I will finish up in this room. After you've washed up, you two can hang out in the living room on your tablets," Karen says, opening one of the photo albums.

The two boys looked at each other, not knowing what to say. They were both scared to enter a room their parents were not in, but they were disgusted with the current situation.

Looking at the boys, Karen knew what was going through their heads. "It will be okay; the bathroom is next to this room. The living room is directly down the stairs. We will be able to see you from here."

"Go ahead, boys. Everything will be okay. There is no such thing as ghosts," Dan says, giving the boys a wink.

The boys hesitantly leave the room; Daniel gets clothes for a shower while Dennis stands in the hallway, waiting for him to finish.

Looking down to the end of the hall, then back to the top of the stairs to his right, Dennis continually scans both sides of the hallway. Looking towards the end of the hall, he sees two more doors leading to rooms that need cleaning. On the right, there is one more door. At the end of the hall, he sees a door that he thinks is probably a closet.

He could hear his mother and father thumbing through the photo albums. His mom was telling him who everyone in the pictures was. Listening to the water from the shower hitting the tub floor, Dennis was getting impatient.

He took quick showers, but his brother. He would stay in there forever if he could.

"Daniel!" Dennis says, knocking on the bathroom door. "Hurry up!"

"I'm almost done!" Daniel shouts back to him.
Looking back to the top of the stairs, Dennis made sure no one or nothing was watching him.

Turning towards the end of the hall, everything looked the same as a minute ago.

"Wait a minute," Dennis thinks to himself. "That door wasn't cracked a while ago."

The last door on the left-hand side had been slightly opened, letting the darkness from inside the room be seen in the hallway. Standing there now, shivering, Dennis watches the door.

With his attention towards the end of the hallway, he hears his mother.

"My God, Dan, what went on in this house?"

Sitting there, speechless, Dan looks at the photo book. It contains photos of little girls, their hands and feet bound by chains.

Taking his hand, Dan reached over and closed the book that Karen was holding. "I don't know Karen, But I think these clothes must be taken to the police station.

Listening in the hallway, Dennis did not know what they had just found. Peering into the bedroom, he sees his mother and father looking at each other in shock.

As Daniel exits the bathroom, all clean from showering. Dennis turns back towards the door down the hall. It was closed completely.

"Don't go downstairs!" Dennis tells Daniel. "Wait for me to shower, and then the two of us will be waiting for Mom and Dad at this door to go downstairs with us."

Daniel looked at him, squinting his eyes, trying to figure out what was happening. Then it hit him, and his eyes widened: "You saw something, didn't you?"

"Just please, wait right here for me," Dennis says, closing the door to take his shower.

Chapter 5

Wicked Dreams

They were finally done after a long day in that bedroom, opening box after box of clothes, old financial records, and the photos Dan and Karen found.

Dennis sat on the couch in the living room as his parents cleaned up after supper. Daniel spent a while in the downstairs bathroom, trying to avoid doing anything else that night. He hadn't slept the night before and was on his last bit of energy. On top of that, he was worrying about tonight and whether he would get any sleep. Or was he going to hear that voice again, that little girl asking him to help her?

Karen enters the living room, where Dennis sits on the couch with his tablet. "We are going to sleep in that bedroom tonight. Let you two have the couches in here."

"Do what!" Dennis answers quickly. "You're going to leave us down here?"

"Dennis, there is nothing in the house. No such thing as ghosts." Karen tells him, grabbing the sheets she had brought to sleep in.

"What about that little girl you saw yesterday?" Dennis asks wide-eyed.

"That was just a figment of my imagination, Dennis. My mind was playing tricks on me," She says, looking at Dan. "Now, don't get me wrong, your dad and I have found some things telling us that my uncle was a bad man. But there is no such thing as ghosts."

"You talking about the photo album you wouldn't let us see? The one you put in the car with the two boxes of clothes?" Dennis asks as Daniel emerges from the bathroom and sits on the other couch.

"Yes, we will take all that to the police tomorrow and see if they know where it came from." She looks at Daniel. "Are you going to be okay sleeping down here? Dennis doesn't like the fact that we're going to make a bed on the floor in that bedroom." Karen continues.

He looked at Dennis and then back at his mother. "Yeah, we should be okay; you're just right there," he said, looking at the top of the stairs. "But it stinks in there."

Karen laughs, "The windows are open, and we pulled the carpet and threw it out the window. There were beautiful hardwood floors under the carpet."

Since it was the first room upstairs, they would only be twenty feet away at most.

"Dennis, they will be right up there," Daniel says, pointing to the first room upstairs.

"We will be okay," Dennis says, giving in to them.

"Goodnight, boys," Dan says, walking upstairs with Karen following behind. "Yeah, goodnight, you two, sweet dreams."

"Why did you agree with them?" Dennis asks Daniel.

Daniel asks Dennis to slide over. They lie beside each other on the couch. "Because you need to see this!" Daniel says, turning his tablet on.

Looking at the image, Dennis sees that he was in the bathroom researching this house. It was a picture of Uncle Richard; the heading of the article read 'Man found dead in his home.' The story says that he tripped over the chest at the foot of their bed. Falling forward, he landed face-first on the base of the mantle, a three stack of bricks all around. It was built for safety, so the fire couldn't accidentally spread to the carpet. Hitting the bricks, it bent his neck backward, breaking it.

"Wow, that's a bad way to die," Dennis says.

"That's not all," Daniel adds. "Look at this."

He minimizes that page and opens another web page. It is a story from a few weeks after his death. It was another man in the community; his name was Henry Fields. He was dying of cancer at the age of sixty-four. He had something he wanted to get off his chest before he died.

He told the reporter a story about him and his friend Richard.

He told how the two of them would go out at night and kidnap little girls.

He told how both of their wives knew about it. They didn't like it but were too scared to do or say anything about it to them or the police.

Henry's wife had already passed, but Richards's wife was still alive. Henry's children were present for the interview. They were shocked to hear the story their dad was telling.

After the interview, the newspaper informed the authorities and printed it in the next day's edition. He had given them some of the children's names; they were children who had gone missing years earlier.

When the police heard about it, they went to Richards's house. But they were too late; he died moments after the interview. The police talked to the children; they told the police that they never heard or known anything of this story their dad had told them.

Without finding any evidence in the house or proof that it was true, they went to Aunt May.

Richard was deceased, and she was the only one left to ask questions.

She told them that she had never heard anything so ridiculous. She knew nothing of this, and she said that he and his wife had been their friends all their lives.

Sickened over the story, the only thing she could come up with was maybe his dementia was getting worse. She told the police that when the children were going missing, Henry and Richard were going out and helping the police look for the people doing it. She told them those memories might be returning to him in his old age, and his mind was twisting them around.

His mind may be confusing him, making him think they did it.

After looking into it for a few more months and not coming up with anything, the police chalked it up to his dementia, making him think they were the ones who had done it.

"Whoa," Dennis says, looking at his brother. "Or maybe he wasn't lying."

Daniel knew exactly what he was talking about — the boxes of clothes in their car.

Karen starts to dream, returning to when they stayed there for Christmas. In the dream, she is awakened by the front door squeaking open. She gets up quietly so as not to disturb anyone else and walks towards the window. Looking over, she sees her parents lying in the bed beside her. At the window, she peeks through the curtains and sees her Uncle Richard walking to the end of the driveway. It was early in the morning; no one else was awake but the two of them. Her uncle stands there in the driveway with a Christmas present in his hand. After standing there for a few moments, he sees a little girl from across the street walking outside and running over to him. She had long, straight black hair; it was the little girl from the pictures. Uncle Richard and the girl stood there momentarily talking; her uncle gave the girl the present. He hugged her, and they parted ways, returning to their houses.

Karen wakes up from the dream. "She was their neighbor." She says to herself, figuring out why she was in pictures with John. "If she was like family, why wasn't I introduced to her as a child? If she was so important to him, why didn't she join the Christmas party that year." Too tired to think more, she laid her head on the pillow and tried to go back to sleep. After a few moments of thinking about that little girl, her tiredness got the best of her, and she was asleep again.

Chapter 6

Return To Shady Acres

The road was covered with water; it had just finished pouring rain as Melissa drove down the highway. She had been driving all day.

Melissa is a student at Penn State; it is an all-day drive home to Macon, Georgia. She wasn't about to waste money on a few hours of sleep in a hotel. She would save her money and drive back to Shady Acres.

Back home, all she had was her mother and her little dachshund. That dog has been part of their family for years. It was the last thing her father gave her before he passed away. She named it Layne; it was her father's middle name.

After crossing the Georgia state line and leaving South Carolina, she saw the sign for the rest area. It was one o'clock in the morning, but she had to use the restroom, and her eyes were starting to go weak from seeing the road all day. She stopped and took a little break to wake up for the rest of the ride home.

Parking her car in the closest spot to the entrance, she is very weary of being alone. She parked in a handicapped spot; at one o'clock in the morning, she did not think someone would say anything. Looking around as she walks towards the restrooms, she searches for a security officer, hoping one is around for protection. There was no one else but her at the rest stop. Or so she thought; looking into the far parking lot on the other side of the facility, she saw a transfer truck with its driving lights on. "Probably someone resting in their truck before they return to the road." She thought.

Entering the bathroom, it smelt like it had been days since anyone had cleaned it. She opens the first stall and sees that the last person there didn't flush. She closes the door and goes to the second one; it has paper all over the floor. Opening the third door is a winner; it is still clean and sanitary. She takes the paper and cleans the seat, not trusting the last person.

She heard the door open after she was finished and about to leave the stall. She stopped dead in her tracks; the footsteps passed her and entered one of the stalls. She listened carefully to every move and heard the person using the restroom. She opens the door with a deep breath of relief and walks towards the sink. Looking into the mirror, she sees that her long, straight hair is tangled from sitting in the car all day. She combed her hand through it, trying to straighten it out. With a disgusted look, she quits trying to fix it, seeing she was making it worse.

When the bathroom stall opened, Melissa's eyes grew wide. It wasn't a woman in the stall like she thought it was. It was a man, and he was looking straight at her with crazed eyes.

"What are you doing in here?" Melissa shouts at him.

"Looking for a party, I think I found one." He says with a grin.

"Don't come near me!" Melissa warned as she pulled out her cell phone.

The man slaps it out of her hands before she can open the home screen. With a quick dash, the man was on her and attempting to push her to the floor.

Melissa held her ground with all her energy, keeping her feet on the ground. She knew it was all over if she went to the cold bathroom floor.

Fighting to get free, she sees a knife sticking out of his pocket. Freeing her hand, she reaches for it. After a couple of tries, she is able to grab the knife.

She cuts his arm, forcing him to release her; the man takes a step back. Before he can regain his focus, Melissa takes the knife and pierces his groin. The man falls to the ground and screams in pain.

Melissa drops the knife and runs to her car; scrambling in her purse for her keys, she continues to hear the man yell from the bathroom.

Stumbling with the keys, she unlocks the car. She turns the ignition over, slams the shifter into reverse, and backs out of the parking space. Now, in drive, the tires spin and squeal like a dragster racing down the strip. Melissa looks into the rear-view mirror to ensure the man isn't following her. There is nothing but a pitch-black sky behind her, but it doesn't stop her. She races down the interstate at ninety miles an hour, getting as far away as fast as possible.

Daniel wakes up around 2 a.m. with a severe headache. He goes upstairs to the bedroom and tugs on his mother's arm.

"Mom, mom. Do you have any aspirin? My head hurts."

"It's in the kitchen on the table," his mother says, tossing in the other direction and falling back asleep.

Daniel tiptoes into the kitchen, not to wake his brother.

He locates the aspirin beside her purse on the kitchen table.

"Yes!" He says to himself, rejoicing over finding the medication that would soon ease his pain.

Taking two out of the bottle, he steps to the sink and pours a glass of water, pops the pills in his mouth, and downs them.

Daniel fills the glass with more water and sips on it as he peers out the kitchen window. In the back of the house is a small shed that they haven't even investigated yet.

"I hope there isn't a bunch of junk in there too!" He says to himself. "That's all we need is more ju…"

"Help me!"

He hears the voice again, and the trembling starts back immediately, as it did the night before.

Looking out the window, he sees a little girl. "Help me!" She looks down at the grass, then back at Daniel. "Help me!"

Daniel drops the glass, breaking it on the floor, and runs back into the living room.

"Why is it only me that keeps hearing this voice?" He asks himself. "Was that the little girl Mama saw?" He continues.

Peeking one bloodshot eye out from the sleeping bag, he sees nothing but darkness.

"Dennis." He says, shaking his brother. "Dennis, wake up."

"What?" Moans a groggy voice from his brother. "What is it? I am trying to sleep." He whispers back.

"Did you hear that?"

"Hear what?" He asks.

"That voice, did you hear it?"

Sitting up quickly, Dennis asks, "Did you hear the voice again?" His eyes widen in fear.

"Yes, and I saw her in the backyard!" Daniel assures him.

Dennis lay down, his eyes searching the room. Daniel went

over and lay with him on the same couch. They both stood on watch for the rest of the night, scared and ready to leave the house.

Melissa finally arrived at her mother's house around four thirty in the morning. Quietly opening the door, she slips into her bedroom and crashes into the bed. Exhausted from the drive and exhausted from the scene at the rest stop. It took no longer than two minutes, and she was fast asleep in the bedroom she grew up in. The place she calls home.

Daylight starts peering into the living room window as Daniel lies wide-eyed and on the defense.

Looking up at the picture on the wall, he sees a picture of his great aunt and uncle. Looking at his Uncle Richard, "Was that story true about you?" he whispers.

Chapter 7

Bright Morning

"Hey, sweetie, I see you made it home!" Melissa's mother says, sitting on the side of her bed and running her hand through her hair. "I missed you so much!"

Melissa lies there, looking up at her mother, smiling. "I missed you too, Mom."

She has longed for her mom to do that for the past few months while she has been away at school.

"So, how has school been?"

"Long and very tough, these classes I have been taking have killed me. It has been hard to keep up with them all."

"It will all be worth it once it's over, sweetie; just hang in there."

Melissa sits up, rubbing her eyes. A glimpse of the man from the night before shoots into her head. The fright of his face springs her to her feet immediately, and she is now wide awake.

"I am starving." She says to her mother as she looks over towards her.

"Are you okay, honey? You looked as if you saw a ghost."

"I'm okay; I don't think I got enough sleep. I will make up for it tonight."

"Okay, well, let's go in the kitchen and see what we can cook for breakfast."

Melissa and her mother both go into the kitchen to find breakfast.

"Honey, will you grab the paper off the front porch for me?" Her mother asks as she opens the refrigerator for eggs.

Melissa walks onto the porch and retrieves the newspaper. She thumbs through it quickly to see if it said anything about the man in the rest area. There was nothing in the paper about it. Sighing with relief, she folds it up to take to her mother. As she turns back towards the door, she glances at the house next door and stops in her tracks. "Whose car is that?" She asks herself. "Was it there last night when I got home?"

Walking back into the house, she finds her mom with a frying pan full of eggs and the smell of toast filling the air.

"Whose car is that next door?" She asks her mother.

"The neighbors told me it was May's niece and her family. They are there to clean the house and get it ready to put on the market."

Melissa peers out the door over at the house once more. "I guess I need to go introduce myself today," she says to herself with a cold look on her face.

Ever since she was four years old, she did not like having to look at that house.

When her sister Danielle walked over there with Richard, Melissa told her parents she was at that man's house.

When they questioned Richard, he told them that Melissa was mistaken and her sister was not there.

Being four years old, they didn't listen to her. They went to the police and had neighbors looking for her. But she was never found, and after a couple of days, Melissa continued to tell them she had gone next door. They finally had the police check their house.

Danielle was not found there, and she was never seen again.

To this day, Melissa can still remember every detail of that day. They were out in the yard playing hide-and-seek, and they were always told to stay in their yard. During this game, her sister disobeyed the rules.

Hiding in their neighbor's yard, Melissa looked for her, calling her name.

She does not find her, but she sees her walking in the back door to the neighbor's house, holding Richard's hand. That was the last time anyone saw her.

Chapter 8

Meeting The Family

"I'm telling you, Mom, this house is haunted!" Daniel insists to his mother as he helps her remove the trash from the master bedroom.

"Daniel, there's no such thing as ghosts. It's all just your imagination."

"But mom!"

"No buts about it, end of story."

"Did you get the door to the pantry unlocked?" Karen asks Dan the minute he enters the bedroom.

Dan looks at her as if he has forgotten to open the door. He turns around and exits the bedroom to investigate it.

"It's not locked; it's just stuck or something," Dan shouts to Karen upstairs, jerking on the door, trying to please his wife by prying it open.

Dennis brings a hammer to his father. "Here, hit the door knob with this, Mom said. Bust the knob and try to remove the lever."
Dan hesitates to take the hammer.

"Dad, a new door knob is only a few bucks. A few bucks

compared to Mom nagging you about the door. Which one do you prefer?"

Dan agrees and takes the hammer from him. Someone knocks on the door as he raises the hammer to hit the doorknob.

"Dan, are you going to get that?" Karen shouts from the bedroom.

"Yes, dear," Dan says, walking towards the door.

He opens the door, and there is a lady with long black hair and a disgusted look.

"Sorry to bother you, sir, so you were kin to the family that lived here?" She says, staring a hole through Dan.

"My wife was their niece. Can I help you with anything?"

"I just wanted to come over and introduce myself," Melissa says, gathering herself and taking the smirk off her face. "I'm sorry, my name is Melissa. I grew up next door." She says, stepping into the house without Dan's approval.

"My name is Dan; this is my son Dennis.

"My other son Daniel and my wife Karen are upstairs cleaning."

Melissa looks around and sees the picture of Richard and May, it is lying on the floor.
"Well, I came over to ask a favor." She says, looking at the picture.

"Not a problem; what do you need?"

"You see that picture on the floor." She says, pointing at it.

"Yeah, that's a photo of my wife's aunt and uncle," Dan tells her.

"I know who they are," Melissa says, staring at him. "Do you know who I am?"

Looking confused, Dan looks at Dennis. Then back up at her. "I'm sorry, I guess I don't."

"I saw Richard take my sister to this house. She was never seen again," Melissa says, staring at Dan.

Both Dan and Dennis look at each other. Dennis is instantly frightened and runs upstairs to where his mother and Daniel are.

"I'm sorry, I don't know what you're talking about." Dan ensures.

"No one ever believed me," she continues. "But I know what I saw. He walked her in through the back door, the last time anyone saw her. I told my parents, they didn't believe me at first. Then, twenty-four hours passed, so they asked the cops to investigate. They didn't find her or proof that she was in the house. My parents spent years looking for her, along with the rest of the town. I told everyone in the neighborhood that she went into this house. But it could never be proven."

Looking at her in disbelief, Karen and the boys came downstairs and stood behind Dan.

"Melissa, is it?" Karen starts, "There is something you need to see. Can you follow me?"

"Yes, ma'am," Melissa says, instantly intrigued at what it could be.

"Dan, go get the things in the car, please."

Hearing his mother, Daniel and Dennis knew they would see the clothes again and maybe what was in the photo album.

As Dan goes to the car, he sees someone parked on the side of the road. When the man sees Dan walking outside, he shifts his vehicle in drive and leaves.

Dan looked at the man; he looked familiar. It didn't take long to remember who he was. He was the man who had squirted the children on the trampoline the day they arrived.

The man continued staring at Dan as he pulled away. He was an older man with round, black eyeglasses and a green and white checkered golf hat.

The look he gave Dan gave him the chills. It was the same look everyone in the neighborhood had given them.

Reaching into the trunk, he grabs the photo album and sets it in one of the boxes.

As he takes the boxes, he
hears another car pull up.

"Hey, sir," The driver says.

Dan sees something he hasn't
seen since they arrived; the man
has a friendly smile — something he
hasn't witnessed in the
neighborhood so far.

"Do you want to know why
all these people are giving you
looks? I can tell you everything,"
he says.

Dan sets the boxes down and
shakes his hand.

"My name is Dan, and yes, I
would love to hear the story.

"My name is George, and I have heard every version of the story."

"Well, come on in, and let's hear it," Dan says.

"One condition," George starts. "I'm not going in that house. We can sit on the back porch, and I will tell you."

Chapter 9

Uncle Richard

Dan gathers chairs from the dining room and sets them in a circle so everyone can face each other.

Dennis listens to crickets and other insects chirping in the woods in the backyard. Sitting on the back patio, he feels one with the woods.

"So I see y'all have found some clothes," George says. "What is the photo album?"

Dan picks up the photo album and hands it to George.

He looks at the first two pages and then hands it back. "I've seen enough."

George presses a button on his tablet, and it lights up. He sits there typing. "I like the tablets with cellular service; I can use them anywhere."

"Yeah, we had to jump our service from our phones to use ours," Dennis tells him.

With everyone sitting around in a circle, George pulls up the page he wants to show them.

He turns it to show everyone, "We looked at that last night." Daniel tells everyone.

It was the piece from the paper on Henry Fields.

"Who is that?" Karen asks the twins.

"It is the man who told the newspaper about kidnapping children and being in on it with your uncle," George tells her. "He had dementia. They investigated it but found nothing and said his mind was confused." He stops talking and looks at everyone. "But he didn't make it up; it was true."

A shocked look appears on Karen's face. "My uncle had something to do with children going missing?"

"Where do you think all those clothes and the pictures came from?" George says, pointing at the evidence sitting in the boxes. "Your aunt wasn't in on it, but she stood by and let it happen, not saying a word."

"When the cops searched the house, why didn't they find these clothes?" Dan asks him.

"Well, Richard died before Henry. After he died, May heard Henry had talked to the newspaper. So she stored everything in the attic."

"Attic?" Dan interrupted.

"Yes, the attic, the fireplace was blocked off in the attic. They loosened some bricks and set the boxes inside to hide them," George continued. "After the house was searched, she returned the boxes from the attic to the bedroom. She wanted it to be found after she had passed. After searching the home, they chalked it up as Henry's mind failed him. She later hired someone to board up the attic."

"Why did she do that?" Karen asks. "If she brought the evidence back into the house, why did she board up the attic?"

"Well," George starts and pauses for a second. "That's where some of the 'things' happened."

Dan and Karen look at each other, then at Melissa.

"What things," Melissa asked, not knowing if she wanted to hear the answer.

George shrugs his shoulders slightly. "You know, the things they did to the girls."

Melissa yells, "Take me to where the attic is boarded up!"

George stands up, puts his hand on her shoulder, and then pushes down. "Sit down, let me finish."

"Take me up there now!" She screams.

"One, I'm not going in there. Two, there is nothing in that attic. It was cleaned out completely before it was sealed off." George assures her.

"Aunt May knew this was going on?" Karen asks in disbelief.

"Yes," George starts. "Your aunt did not want any part of it. When she and Richard met, he wasn't like this. It started years after they were married. I don't know exactly how it started; I only know that he became friends with Henry, and it all started. He threatened your aunt if she ever told anyone about it. He and Henry may get arrested, but there were more people involved. It was a whole ring of men all over this part of the state. Both your Aunt May and Henry's wife Susanne were warned. If they ever told anyone, they would be killed. Your aunt was in fear for a long time. She would hear them in the attack, listening to the muffled screams of the girls. I guess she grew numb after all the years of witnessing everything. After your uncle died, she was embarrassed about it and just wanted to hide everything. At least hide it until she passed away. That's why she left the evidence out, for someone to find after she was gone." George explains to her.

Karen is disgusted, "Too bad my uncle couldn't have died a more painful death. He fell over, knocked himself out, and never woke up. Died from a broken neck."

George laughs and shakes his head as he looks down at the ground.

"What's that about?" Melissa asks, getting upset because this conversation had no reason for laughter.

"Sorry, it's because of the way he died. Everybody thinks he just tripped." George says, putting his tablet on the ground beside him.

The twins sit there during the conversation, letting all of this sink in with their mouths wide open.

"He didn't trip," George starts. "Your Aunt May killed him."

Karen looks at him with confusion, "Killed him?"

"Yes, it is true that he fell and hit the corner of the mantle, breaking his neck. But it wasn't an accident; your Aunt May drugged his drink with sleeping pills. They both took sleeping pills, but your aunt gave him a triple dose that night. It hit him when he was getting ready for bed. As he approached the bed, he saw that she had her sleeping pills out on the nightstand. Your aunt saw that he was starting to figure it all out. She quickly pushed him and retrieved her gun from the nightstand. But she didn't need it, when she pushed him, he fell and hit his head on the fireplace and broke his neck. After she saw what happened, she called the police." George turns his attention to Karen. "The kicker is, they both took the same sleeping medicine, and both had prescriptions. So when they found it in his system, they thought nothing of it. They figured he accidentally took too much and overdosed. There were never any suspects; it was written up as an accident."

Everybody sits there momentarily, silent and letting it all sink in.

After a few moments, "So how do you know all of this?" Dan asks.

They see a shadow approach from around the side of the house, and George leans back in his chair. He folds his hands behind his head in a Relaxing motion. "Because it wasn't a two-person group in this neighborhood. It was a three-person group."

The shadow has reached fifteen feet from them. They see the person's arm raise, and he points something at them. They hear the hammer of a gun as it gets pulled back and into position.

Dan sees the older man who was parked on the side of the road earlier.

"Everyone, meet my father, Walter," George says. "When your aunt died, she left everything in her house to be found. Once found, with evidence these days. They could find my father's prints on the photos and clothes. We can't have that."

"Take them!" Karen says quickly. "Just let us go; we won't say a word!"

Walter approaches the group and stands by George; both laugh at the suggestion.

"You know we can't do that," George says as he takes a gun from his father.

"Come on, let's go in the house," George motions the end of his pistol towards the back door.

George and Walter follow the group into the house.

"Did I scare you last night, little boy?" Walter asks Dennis. "That was me in that bedroom with the door cracked. I was watching to make sure y'all didn't find anything. That's when I found out what y'all found! I have been trying to get into this house and remove everything. But normally, no one can get close to this property without someone seeing it. Everybody keeps their eyes out. But last night, everyone in the neighborhood was focused on the bedrooms where the lights were on. The rooms all of you were in. I went around the backyard and used the old ladder by the shed. I climbed into the room and listened to everything that was said."

In the house, George made them line up against the wall. "Stay right here."

Dan sees Walter go into the utility room. Emerging out from the dark room, he holds an axe.

"Here," he says as he hands it to George.

George stands there, looking at it for a second, then, with wild eyes, raises it, ready to swing. Karen starts to scream, and the rest look at George in fear.

George turns to face the axe towards the pantry door, the one Dan couldn't open and starts breaking it down. It takes him five swings until it is broken up enough to open.

When he walks into the room, it is so dark that they can no longer see him. But they hear what seems to be a door on the floor open.

"Let's go," George says, walking out of the pantry, making a hand motion, and telling them to start moving.

In a single-file line, Dan was first, followed by Daniel and Dennis. Then Karen and Melissa ended the line.

George throws a flashlight down at the bottom of the basement. "Hand over all the phones." He tells them.

Walking down the steps, they were overwhelmed by the

stench of decay, old iron plumbing, and mold. As they went down, they clenched their noses one by one.

Dan sees the flashlight lying on the ground, revealing that the floor is dirt.

Dan shines it around to show him the surroundings. "Oh my God." He whispers as he looks around.

Throughout the basement, he sees an old bed with chains welded to the headboard and footboard. There is a vertical platform with two small holes on each side and a larger hole in the middle. He knows that this platform was used to lock the children's arms and heads.

There was another table with multiple straps made into it, again to hold someone motionless.

He quickly figured out that these were all the instruments they had in the attic at one time. What they used on the girls they kidnapped.

Karen and Melissa looked around with their hands over their mouths. They also knew what everything was used for. In the far corner, there was a large cedar chest. They opened it and saw all their torture instruments: small daggers, a medieval-style flail, larger knives, multiple-size sticks, and a few old whips.

From the door above them, they heard George. "Y'all don't get too comfortable. You see the brick wall to the right?" He sees Dan shine the light in that direction. "You see how that brick looks newer than the rest? That's because that isn't part of the original foundation. All the children's bodies are buried in there."

They all gasp in horror; they hear George laugh. Then he shuts the door and locks the padlock.

Chapter 10

The Spirits Wake Up

They sit on the steps as Dan shines the flashlight towards the brick wall. They are all thinking the same thing. How long was the flashlight going to last?

Walter and his son George are looking for anything else that would prove what happened in the past.

"I still can't believe you were part of this," George tells his father as he looks through the first bedroom on the left.

In the second bedroom, May disassembled the beds that were previously in both bedrooms and stacked them against the wall. The dressers were placed to hold the bed posts and rails against the wall.

Other than those items, the only things in that room were some of May's old clothes that she no longer wore before she died. They were hung up in the closet.

The room smelled of old mattresses and mothballs. He and Walter knew that the door to that room hadn't been opened in a long time.

Looking out of the bedroom window, he saw the neighbor

standing in her driveway. She was searching for Melissa.

"Either we need to finish this quickly or throw this woman with the rest of them," Walter says, turning to George. "Melissa's mother is outside looking for her."

George walks over and looks out the window. "If she knocks on the front door, she will go down there too."

They move to the last bedroom on the left. Opening the door, George saw the fireplace that killed Richard years ago.

The bed was an old four-post mahogany style. George grabbed the rounded top of a post. "So, this is where she killed him." George looked at the floor of the bed and saw the cedar chest stained to match the dark brown finish of the furniture.

Walter searches through the dresser drawers for any other kind of evidence.
Finding nothing, he moves to the closet.

George walks into the bathroom and searches the area.

Melissa opens the chest and retrieves the flail. "If they're stupid enough to leave these down here. I will at least have one ready for when they come back."

Dan grabs a whip, "That is if they come back."

The twins both grab a dagger as Karen grabs a large knife at the bottom of the pile.

"Well, I guess the two boxes of clothes and the photo album were all that was left in the house. The rest is in the basement," Walter says as he takes one more look into the living room.

Standing there watching his father, George finally decides to ask him. "Why were you even part of this?"

Walter turns and looks at him.

"I mean when you told me about this a couple of years ago. I was speechless, and I didn't talk to you for months. The stories you told me were disgusting. Then, after Mom died, I still did not want anything to do with you." George stops and watches the headlights of a car pass by from the living room window. "But I didn't want to see you get caught and have to spend the rest of your life in jail. The other two escaped any trouble and were able to die without anyone knowing. I wanted the same for you, but once you're gone, whatever is found out, there isn't anyone left to arrest." But now, trying to hide your secrets. I am involved; I can go to jail." He points his finger to the basement door. "I can go for kidnapping."

"No one is going to find out it was us," Walter says now, standing directly in front of George as he sits on the couch.

"How is that dad? How is no one going to find out? George asks.

"Because we are about to burn this house to the ground with them in it," Walter says with no emotion on his face.

"We are going to do what!" George asks, raising his voice. "We are not killing them!"

"Calm down, George, after all the children I helped kill.

Adding five more people isn't that big of a deal."

Walter walks out the front door as George stands in the living room in disbelief at what his father said. He is stuck in position and cannot move.

George hears rustling outside. His father walks back into the house, holding a gasoline canister in each hand. He lays one beside George and the other in the kitchen. "Get started," he tells George.

Walter exits the house again, and after a few moments, he re-enters the house with a woman in his arms. It was Melissa's mother; she was unconscious with blood running down her face.

"What happened to her!" George screams.

"She was looking for her daughter while I got the gas cans. So I hit her with the butt of my gun." Walter takes her to the basement door. "Open the door," he tells George.

George looks into his father's eyes. Even though he was older now. George was still frightened by the look he was giving him.

Without saying a word, he unlocks the padlock. He opens the door, and his father lies her head first on the stairs.

As Dan's flashlight shines toward them. They see

Mellissa's mother slowly slide down the steps.

"Mom!" Melissa screams as she drops her weapon and runs up the steps to catch her.

As the commotion continues below, George shuts the door. Walter picks up a gas can. George looks at the padlock, then back at his dad. With Walter not paying attention, he lays the lock to the side, leaving the basement door shut but not locked.

Walter walks into the living room, pouring gas everywhere. "Pick up the other can!" He yells to George.

George picks up his can and slowly walks into the

kitchen. He does not want to do this, but seeing how his father is acting, he knows if he doesn't, he may end up down there with the rest of them.

Slowly, he started pouring the gas into the kitchen; the smell instantly gave him a headache.

He was pouring it throughout the kitchen, and from the corner of his eye, he saw his father slowly approaching him. He was walking backward from the living room.

Watching him, wondering what he was doing. He sees him drop the gas can and bring his hands halfway up like surrendering to someone.

George lays his gas can on the ground, seeing multiple objects from the living room.

As his eyes widen in horror, he sees children entering the kitchen. Walter is focused on what he sees rather than where he is in the house. He walks backward and enters the room with the trap door.

Watching these children, George sees that they are covered in blood and have dirt smeared all over their clothes. But those two details don't affect him as much as the third and most important one. They are not actual children; they are more like silhouettes. He can see the children clearly but can also see through them.

George did not believe in ghosts until tonight.

There were twelve in total. They stopped and turned their heads in unison towards George. He stood there in fright, unable to move. They turned their heads and focused on Walter once again.

"You will pay for what you did!" They all whispered at the same time to Walter.

Melissa laid her mother on the ground.

They surrounded her as she shook her mother, trying to wake her.

She comes to and moans in pain and puts her hand up to her head. Wiping her head, she sees the blood.

"That man... He hit me." She says.

"Are you okay, mama?" Melissa says, hugging her.

"Who is that man? Was it Walter?" Her mom asks.

Melissa starts. "Yes! He is one of the ones that took..."

The sounds of wood cracking interrupt her train of thought.

They see light coming through cracks in the center of the door.

They hear more cracking and see more light.

"Someone is standing on that door!" Dan says as he jumps up and grabs his weapon.

They get their weapons ready to attack whoever is about to break through that door.

As Walter stands in horror, looking at the spirits of each of the children. He remembers the nights they killed each one.

He did not feel the wooden door cracking below his feet. He sees

George frozen in fear. "Do something!" He shouts.

George looks at him, then looks toward the back door. "I'm sorry!" He shouts.

Turning towards the door, he hears it lock. Then, the large pantry beside the door suddenly slides in front of it. Looking back in horror, he sees the dead children's spirits. They are looking at him, smiling.

The spirits opened the silverware drawer. A large chef's knife floated out and behind George. The drawer closes, and the knife handle presses against the drawer. The tip of the blade faces George's back.

Three of the spirits turned from Walter and slowly started towards

George. Seeing them, George slowly started stepping back towards the blade.

After a few steps, the spirits suddenly screamed and were instantly in George's face. In horror, George frantically turns. With Nowhere to run, the motion sends him straight into the knife.

Falling, he grabs his chest. With the pain excruciating, he grabs the handle. But is unable to muster up the energy needed to remove the knife.

In his last moments of life, all he could do was look up at the spirits one final time in disbelief.

Now that George is dead, all the spirits focus on Walter again.

"No! Please, no!" He shouts as his legs tremble even more from witnessing what happened to his son.

The spirits move closer and crowd around the pantry entryway.

The spirits forced the door to break. As he hears the wood snap, Walter looks at the spirits in fear.

Walter stares at the spirits as he is falling. The steps broke his body, hearing his leg snap and his shoulder. His old bones couldn't handle this kind of abuse. He was lying on the dirt floor in pain. There is another painful sensation he is feeling. He no longer sees the spirits at the top of the steps. Lying there, he feels continuous punches into his side.

As his neck hurts from the fall, he turns his head slightly to see what this sensation is. There is a large dagger piercing him. He sees Melissa stand up with blood on her hands.

"That's for my sister." She says, staring into his eyes.

She removes the knife from his side and screams in frustration. "Would you die!"

She thrushes the dagger down with all of her might and stabs him in the throat. His trachea is ripped open. Walter clenched his throat, but there was no way he could close it to allow himself to breathe.

Dan quickly grabs Melissa and pulls her back, away from him.

She did not fight Dan; the damage was done. She sat there and watched Walter slowly die.

Karen rushes the twins upstairs; in the kitchen, they see Gerald lying there dead. She turns them the other way and rushes them through the living room and out the front door. She smells the gas and screams. "Get out of the house!"

After watching Walter die, Melissa helps her mother up the stairs. Reaching the kitchen, they see George lying there dead. She didn't know how he died, but she knew both men got what they deserved.

Dan stays in the basement for a moment, still in disbelief at what the men did to those children.

He focuses on the foundation that held the bodies. "I'm sorry for what these men did to each of you. May you rest peacefully. We will have the authorities remove your bodies from this house. They will give you appropriate burial grounds and services."

Dan walks up the steps, and when he reaches the top, he hears a whisper behind him: "Thank you."

He stopped for a second, his heart racing again from the voice. He thought back to his wife seeing someone and his boys hearing someone asking for help. He did not believe them, but now he heard the voice.

As soon as his heart raced, it slowed down. The voice said thank you in a pleasant manner.

"You're welcome, children." He tells them as he leaves the basement to reunite with his family upstairs.

Seeing George lying there, he wondered if it was the work of Walter or the spirits.

Chapter 11

The conclusion

As they gather in the front yard, Daniel hits Dennis in the shoulder.

"Look!" He whispers, pointing to the house.

They watch the spirit of a little girl walk through the living room. She stands at the glass door and stares at the group in the yard.

Everyone turns and looks; their eyes are locked in on the spirit.

"Oh my God!" Melissa says.

Her mother puts her hand to her mouth, and tears fall from her cheeks. "Mandy!" she says faintly. "My sweet child!"

The spirit leans her hands on the glass door. "Mama."

Her voice wasn't a child's; it sounded from another dimension, and its rapid pitches startled everyone.

Mandy's spirit gathers with the other spirits in the living room.

As everyone stands outside watching, they see a lamp fall over. The bulb explodes, and the spark ignites the gasoline that was poured onto the floor.

"Oh no!" Melissa screams.

Dan grabbed her as she started to run towards the house. "It's what they want." He says to her. "Their bodies will be found in the basement, behind that brick wall. We will bury each one of them the proper way."

Dan stares into the roaring blaze, "As far as the house, it needs to be wiped off the face of the earth."

They all stand there and watch the house burn as neighbors pour onto the street. In the distance, they could hear the ambulances and fire trucks approaching, along with the police. The lights were flashing everywhere, and the sirens were piercing their ears.

As the firefighters fought the flames, Karen told the police what happened. She started with the history and the children and then told them what unfolded that night.

They cleared the lot off over the next few days and found all the bones. They were sent to the lab to be identified. They found some instruments in the basement that the fire did not destroy. They were logged in as evidence at the police station.

Karen contacted the insurance company, which reimbursed her for the home. They had the lot cleared but did not plan to sell it. They wanted it to stay an empty lot indefinitely.

The authorities discovered who each child was. Eleven of the twelve were kidnapped from out of state. They didn't live within five hundred miles of the house. Mandy was the only local child they kidnapped. She was from next door.

Melissa, her mother, and all the remaining family members of the children who were still alive had one funeral for them all. They were buried beside each of their already deceased family members. Now, being truly at rest, the families were saddened to hear how they died. But were at peace knowing they now knew where their bodies lay.

Karen and Dan started talking to each other more. Dan started disciplining the boys as he should have. They all started helping their mother around the house. After being stuck in that basement, they no longer took life for granted. It brought them closer together as a family.

In their will, Dan and Karen instructed the boys never to sell the property. It must be continued to be handed down to each generation. Never to be built on or sold to anyone outside of the family.

They left strict instructions for that piece of property to never have any kind of structure erected on it.

As the spirits reunited with their families in the cemetery, they never walked the earth again. Nor did they ever have to walk inside that house they died in, either. They were finally at rest.

Made in the USA
Columbia, SC
19 May 2024

35451353R00083